This annual belongs to

_____

Printed and published in Great Britain by D. C. THOMSON & CO., LTD.
185 Fleet Street
London EC4A 2HS

www.chuggington.com
© Ludorum plc 2010

ISBN 978-1-84535-437-4

ANNUAL 2011

Contents

Wheels to the rails!

The trainees of Chuggington love to ride the rails! Can you see Wilson, Koko and Brewster? Which colour tunnel will the trainees be using today?

Switching signals

The trainees are practising how to change the tracks. Follow the track arrows to see where they are going!

Chugger spotting

Morgan is having a busy day with the chuggers.
Can you count how many times
he has seen each trainee?

Brewster

Koko

Wilson

Koko

CHUGGA CHUGGA CHOO CHOO!

Koko loves to discover new places and is always ready for a chug-a-chug adventure!

Koko is very fast. She likes to zoom along the rails.

She's an adventurous electric engine!

Maintenance yard

Can you join the rivets 1-10 to complete Wilson?
Now colour Wilson in!

BREWSTER GOES BANANAS

One morning, Dunbar was teaching the trainees how to pick up sacks of post without stopping. They couldn't wait for training to start!

Vee interrupted training to ask Brewster to take bananas to the safari park. Peckham the dog wanted to go too!

"Door open... net out...scoop!" Wilson was practising picking up the mail sack.

At the safari park, Mtambo told Brewster about a strange mystery. Bananas had gone missing in the night!

While they were talking, a monkey ran across and jumped into Brewster's boxcar.

As they were chugging back to the depot, Brewster and Peckham kept hearing strange banging noises.
Then suddenly a banana landed on Peckham's head!

At the training yard, it was Koko's turn to practise picking up the mail sack.
"Picking up mail is traintastic" she said smiling.

"Let's go and see what happens to the mail at the sorting office," Dunbar said.
"Wahay! Let's ride the rails!" Wilson called as they rode away.

Brewster headed straight to the maintenance yard to see if Morgan could find out about the strange noises. All Morgan could find were bananas, but as Brewster was leaving the strange noises started again.
"Honking horns!" he said.

After Morgan checked Brewster out, Brewster went to the training yard to practise with the mail sack. Just as he was about to scoop it up, the bag disappeared!

Funny things were happening to Old Puffer Pete too. As Lori was polishing his fenders, a banana skin flew through the air and landed on top of his whistle!

Brewster realised odd things had happened since the safari park. He asked Eddie to leave his lunch out and hide. Sure enough a monkey appeared! Eddie quickly caught it before it could run away with his lunch.

"How did you know it was a monkey?" Hodge asked, as Brewster got ready to take the cheeky culprit home. "Who likes bananas best?" Brewster replied. "Monkeys!"

Copy and colour

Copy this picture of Old Puffer Pete into the grid on the next page, using the lines as a guide. Then colour Pete in!

Brewster

HONKING HORNS!

Brewster takes pride in pulling full carts along the tracks. He is very strong!

Brewster is a brave blue trainee.

Everyone in Chuggington knows they can count on Brewster. He makes sure he finishes his jobs on time.

 22

Wilson

Wilson gets excited about learning new things and loves to train with his friends.

Wilson is a lively red trainee.

He has trainloads of enthusiasm and is always ready to help.

23

Training time!

**The trainees are practising for the mail run.
How many sacks did each trainee catch?**

Koko caught

Wilson caught

Brewster caught

Paint shop

Draw a line to connect each chugger to their paint colours. They may need more than one colour!

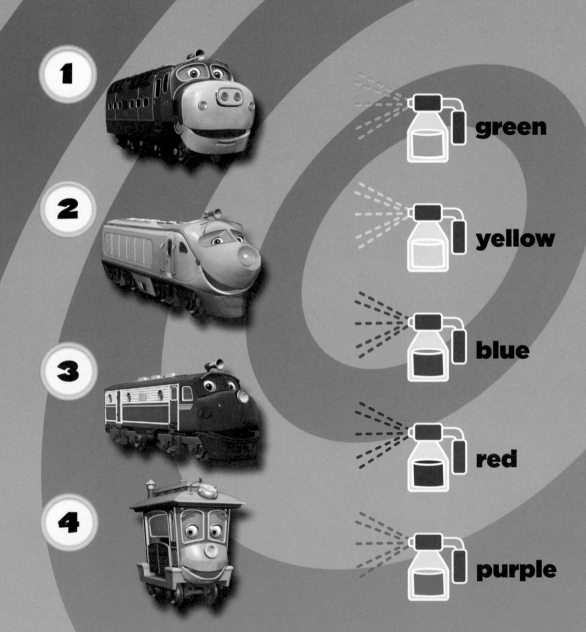

1

2

3

4

green

yellow

blue

red

purple

Making tracks

Will you draw tracks to connect each trainee to their destination?

Koko is going to the timber yard.
Wilson is going to the mountains.
Brewster is going to the safari park.

Let's ride the rails

Follow the track to the depot, answering the questions along the way.

Start

1

Which colour tunnel is Vee asking you to take? Colour in the correct board.

red	blue	green

2

Where does Mtambo work as a guide? Circle the correct location.

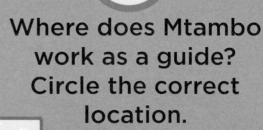

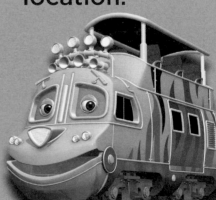

How many cows are in the field? Trace the correct number.

What does Frostini like to make? Circle the correct answer.

3

4

5

What does Koko say? Circle the correct phrase.

Wahay!

Honking horns!

Traintastic!

Finish

KOKO AND THE TUNNEL

One day, Koko found a new tunnel she had never been in before. She wanted to explore, but Vee told her that there were important things to learn before trains could go down tunnels by themselves.

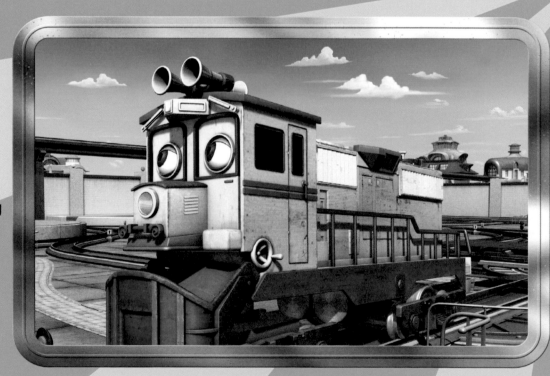

At the training yard, Dunbar was teaching the chuggers how to switch tracks.

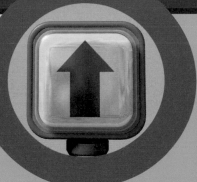

"Once you leave the depot, you have to switch the tracks yourselves," he said, but none of the trainees could get the tracks to switch.

Dunbar got called away by Vee. Brewster suggested that the trainees keep on practising, but Koko and Wilson wanted to explore the tunnel.
"Scaredy chugger!" Koko teased as she left with Wilson.

After a while, Wilson wanted to go back to the depot. "No way!" Koko said. "We need to see what's on the other side of the tunnel!"

"I want to go home..." Wilson whined as he followed Koko deeper into the countryside.
"Ok, we'll find somewhere to turn," Koko said.

When they came to switch track they couldn't change the switch. Koko decided to drive fast towards the switch, thinking it would help, but that was wrong!

With a loud clatter, she zoomed off the rails and landed on the ground. "Oh no, I can't move!" koko moaned.

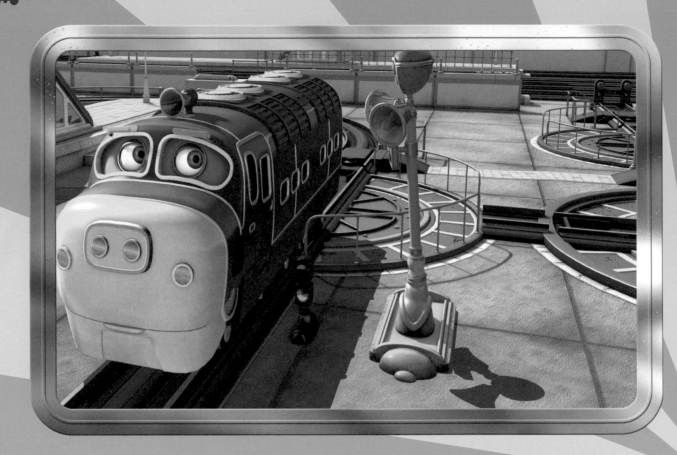

It was taking them
far too long and
Brewster was starting
to worry about his
friends. He asked Vee
if Calley could help
look for them.

After a long search, Calley found the trainees and winched Koko back onto the track.
"From now on, I'm not going anywhere until I know how to be safe on the rails!" Koko said.

"I'm sorry I made you so worried today, Brewster," Koko told her friend when they were getting ready to sleep at the roundhouses. "I'm lucky to have a traintastic friend like you."

Spot the difference

Can you spot the five differences between
these two chugger pictures?
Tick a box when you find each one!

1 ☐

2 ☐

3 ☐

4 ☐

5 ☐

Colour the chugger

Which chugger is this? Colour by number to find out!

Dunbar

LET'S GET THOSE WHEELS TO THE RAILS!

Dunbar is a very clever chugger.

He teaches the trainees everything they need to know about how to be good chuggers.

Dunbar is always ready to buckle up the trainees to the right rolling stock for the job.

Old Puffer Pete

Oh, Ho, Ho!

Old Puffer Pete has worked in Chuggington for 150 years!

He is very wise and full of helpful advice.

Pete is a steam engine that likes to go slow and steady, otherwise he gets overheated.

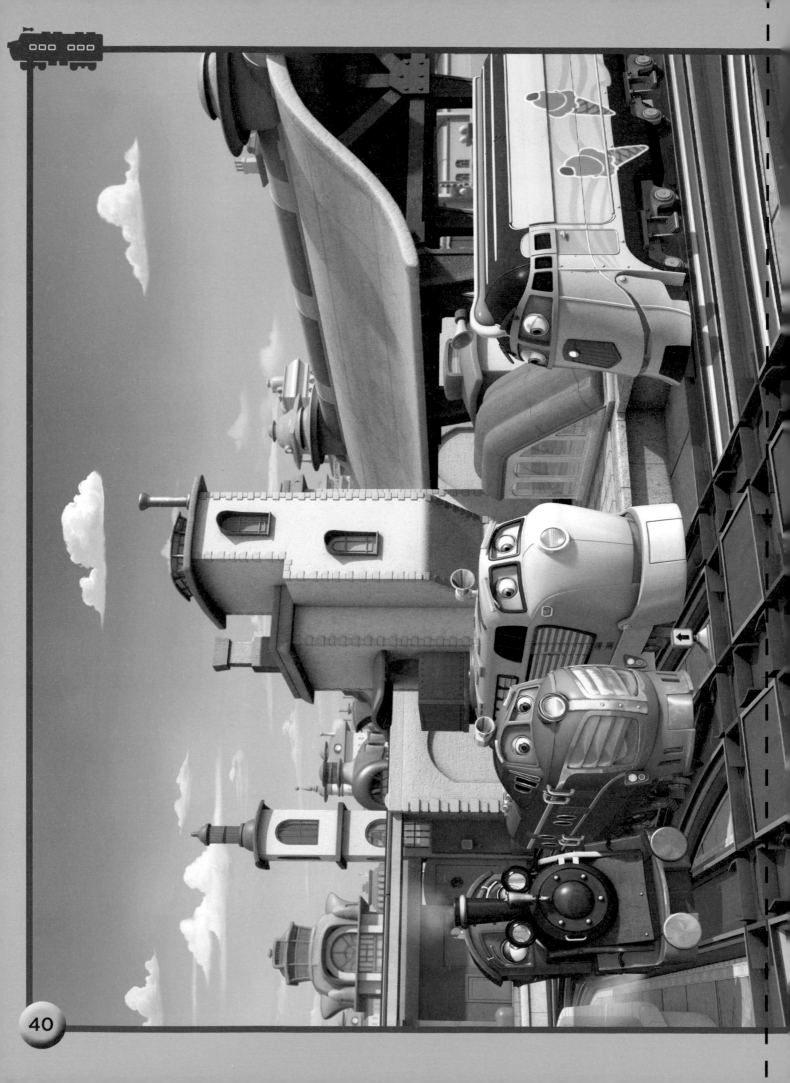

Let's race!

Lori is taking pictures of the chuggers racing, but they are training so fast, the photos are blurred! Can you draw lines to match a name to each picture?

Koko

Brewster

Wilson

Harrison's maze

Harrison is ready to start a night run, but which way should he go to get to the quarry? Guide him through the maze.

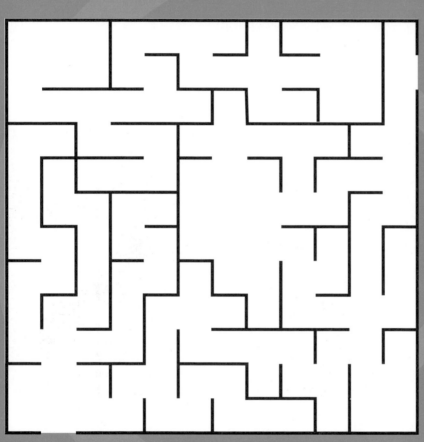

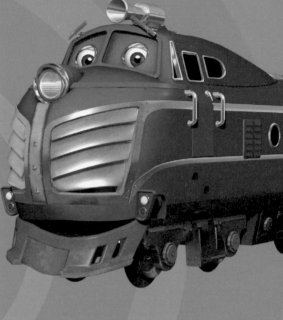

Harrison is the fastest chugger in Chuggington!

Chugger puzzle

Ask an adult to cut out the squares, then mix up the pieces and see if you can make this picture, and the picture on the other side!

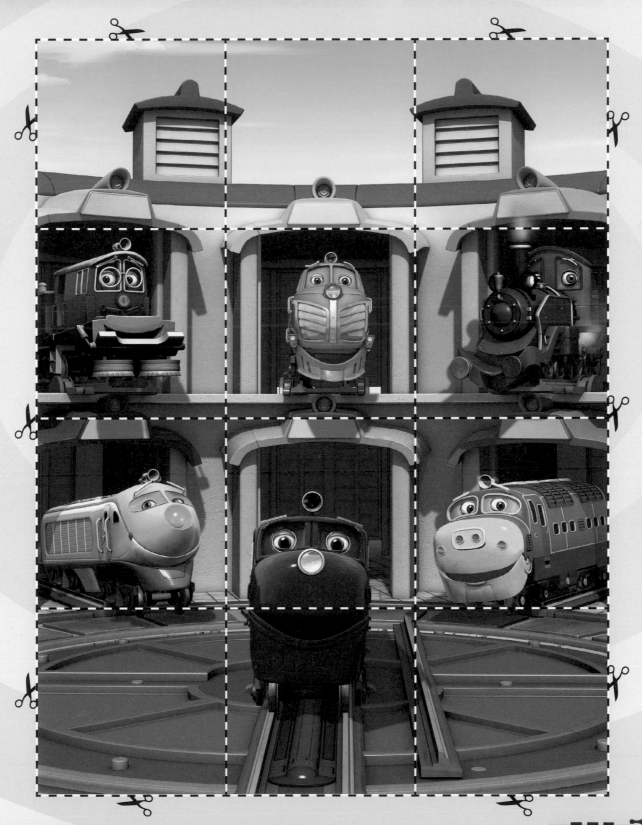

43

Chugger puzzle

Which track?

Which colour track will take Wilson and Brewster to the quarry?

Safari search

CAN YOU FIND?

Can you spot everything at the safari park?

Ebo

Vicki

Dr Gosling

monkey

bananas

giraffe

Mtambo

Tick off everything you find!

47

One morning, Vee asked Koko to go to the timber yard. "I can't wait! I'm ready for my tunnel colour Vee," Koko said excitedly.

"Aren't you forgetting something Koko?" Vee said. Just then, Old Puffer Pete rolled up to the platform, ready to get his tunnel colour too.

"Watch the board for your tunnel colour," Vee said. "But I was here first," grumbled Koko.

"When I was your age, this was all done with coloured flags," Pete said. Koko rolled her eyes. She had heard that story before.

"Is it my turn now?" Koko asked with relief when Pete had gone towards the green tunnel. "Koko, haven't you forgotten something?" asked Vee. "Your flatcar to carry the timber!" "Back in two clickety-clacks," Koko called.

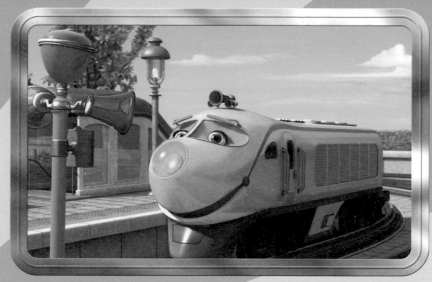

At the rolling stock yard Koko was too excited to buckle up the flatcar. Dunbar helped Koko by saying, "Back up slooowly."

"Traintastic! I'm going to chug-a-chug all the way to the timber yard and then chug-a-chug to the paper mill!"

Meanwhile, Old Puffer Pete was enjoying his trip, when two squirrels jumped onto his roof.
"Oh! Hello Mr Squirrel," he said.

The large squirrel brushed his tail on Pete making the old chugger laugh. "Ho, ho, that tickles!" he chuckled before chugging away.

Koko's tunnel colour was announced. It was green! "That's the same as Old Puffer Pete's tunnel," she said. "I don't want to get stuck behind Old Puffer Pete. This is too much of an adventure to go slow," she said as she sped away.

Koko raced out of the tunnel. "Woo-hoooo!" she shouted, zipping round the bend. "Go Koko, go Koko."

"Watch out Mr Squirrel!" she called, zooming past the squirrels jumping across the tracks.

Soon Koko had caught up with slow moving Old Puffer Pete. She switched tracks and zoomed around him.

"Slow and steady!" called Pete, but Koko didn't pay attention.

Koko collected her load of timber and raced to the paper mill. Suddenly, she saw a baby squirrel on the tracks!

"Emergency stop!" Koko slammed on her brakes. The squirrels hurried away. "I'm sorry, I was going too fast. I didn't mean to scare you."

Old Puffer Pete had been right; she should have been going slow and steady. "How am I going to pick up these logs?" Koko said.

Just then, Pete came around the corner. "Old Puffer Pete you were right," Koko said. "I was going fast and I spilt my load!" Old Puffer Pete helped lift the logs back on to Koko's wagon. "Old Puffer Pete to the rescue!" he said, smiling at Koko.

"Thanks, Pete!" Koko said, when he had finished putting all the logs back onto her flatcar.

"I'm worried about the squirrels on the tracks," she said. So Koko and Pete used a log to make a bridge between the trees.
"Traintastic! They love it!" Koko said happily.

As Koko and Old Puffer Pete returned to the depot, Koko said, "Now I've learnt to always take it slow and steady."
"Whoa-ho-ho. Sometimes it's good to let off some steam," Pete said. "Last one home has square wheels!"

Odd one out

Which picture of Hodge and Eddie is the odd one out?

Colour the chugger

Which chugger is this?
Colour him in!

Zephie

I LOVE TO SPIN!

Zephie loves to spin around and scissors up and down when she is excited.

Zephie is a green scissor-lift trolley.

She is Chuggington's most cheerful chugger.

Emery

MADE YOU LOOK MADE YOU STEER!

Emery is a passenger train that zips all over Chuggington.

He likes to play and laugh as he works.

Emery speeds around the depot with a funny joke for anyone he sees.

Chugger patterns

What comes next in each sequence?

Shadow shapes

Which shadow matches each chugger?
Draw a line to connect the pairs.

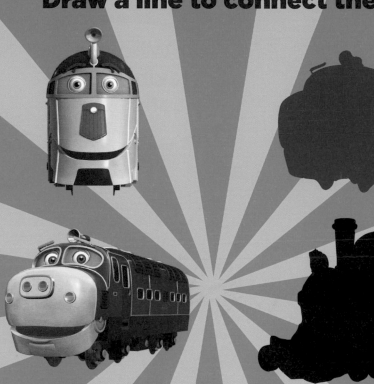

Hide and seek

Wilson is hiding in the depot! Can you find him?
What else can you spot?

Fast find

- ✓ **Action Chugger**
- ✓ **Dunbar**
- ✓ **Zephie**
- ✓ **Vee**

Can you find Morgan?

✓

Where is the clock tower? What time is it?

✓

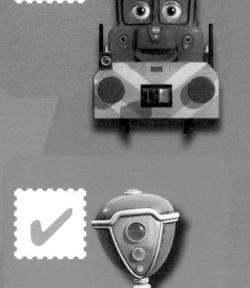

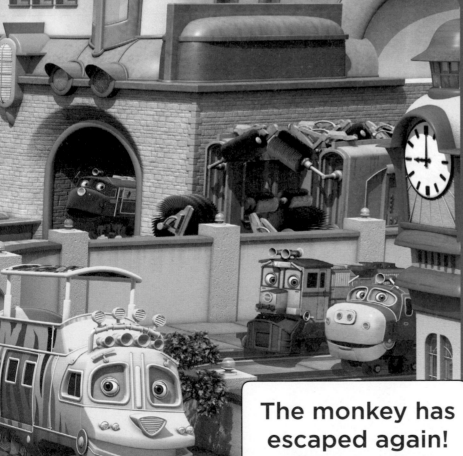

✓

The monkey has escaped again! Where is he?

Pete's name game

Old Puffer Pete keeps getting the names of the trainees wrong. Who does he mean? Can you connect the name to the trainee?

WILSON

BREWSTER

KOKO

DEWSTER

WILBER

COOKIE

Missing letters

Will you complete each chugger's name?
Connect the dots to reveal the answers.

Zephi_   Zephie

_ee   Vee

Ol_in   Olwin

Harri_on   Harrison

C_atsworth   Chatsworth

Emer_   Emery

63

Spot the difference

Can you spot the five differences between these two chugger pictures? Tick a box when you find each one.

1
2
3
4
5

Which part?

Can you connect the right part to each chugger?

HODGE AND THE MAGNET

One morning, Chuggington was running very slowly. The yellow line was down and it was causing all kinds of problems around Chuggington!

Dunbar told the trainees to make themselves useful around the depot. "We can do that!" cried Wilson.

Hodge and Calley got ready to mend the track.
"You'll need the magnet to pick up the track," Calley said.
"Just have to get Eddie," replied Hodge, and they set off to collect him.

Eddie was no where to be found. Hodge went to the repair shed to wait. Emery pulled up, however only Lori got off.
"Oh rivets! He must be running late again," said Hodge.

Just then, Wilson appeared and asked what the problem was. Hodge explained that he was waiting for Eddie, as he had to guide the magnet.
"I can help you!" Wilson cried. "C'mon! Let's ride the rails," he said, and they raced away.

"It's busy today, isn't it Morgan?" said Zephie as they watched the chuggers line up.
"Poor Vee's got her work cut out," Morgan replied.
Morgan told Vee that Eddie had gone to repair the track, not realising Eddie wasn't with Hodge or Wilson.

Hodge nervously approached the broken track with Wilson.
"I wish Eddie was here. I'm relying on you Wilson, because I can't see," Hodge said as he got in to place to pick the track up.

"Eddie always helps me line up the magnet." Hodge said. "But I can help," said Wilson. "Oh, look, there's a butterfly!" "Pay attention! We have got a job to do," said Hodge. "Sorry, I'm ready."

Wilson tried hard to direct Hodge and the magnet. But it was really difficult and the magnet kept missing the rails. "Up a bit Hodge...down a teensy little bit...back a bit..." Wilson said. "Aargh! Wilson! You need to be clear," Hodge said.

"Clunk!" Wilson had moved too close and the magnet was now stuck on his face!
"I never should have let you talk me in to this!" said Hodge.

After a lot of pulling, Hodge finally managed to get the magnet off Wilson's face by turning it off.
"I can't fix the track. Let's just go back," he said, feeling sad.
"You can do it, Hodge," said Wilson. "Let's try again."

Hodge swung the magnet around again, catching a track and moving it out of place.

"I can't do this," said Hodge.

"Yes you can, you just need to turn the magnet off when you're not using it. I know you can do it," said Wilson.

Within moments Wilson and Hodge had put the track back in place.

"Perfecto!" said Wilson with excitement.

Eddie appeared just in time to see the chuggers finishing their job.

"Well done, Hodge, you saved the day!" he said.

Through the tunnel

Which tunnel will take Zephie to the farm?

RED

BLUE

YELLOW

GREEN

Matching pairs

Can you draw lines to match the chuggers?

Frostini

IT'S COLD, IT'S YUMMY!

Frostini is an Italian ice-cream chugger.

Speak Italian like Frostini:

Yes is Si
Say "See"

Thank you is Grazie
Say "Grat-zee"

Frostini likes to play with different flavours and make new recipes.

74

Mtambo

I'LL TELL YOU A STORY...

He gives tours to visitors wanting to see the different animals in the park.

Mtambo has travelled all around the world and always has a good adventure story to tell.

Mtambo is the safari park ranger engine.

Copy and colour

Copy this picture of Hodge into the grid on the next page, using the lines as a guide. Then colour him in!

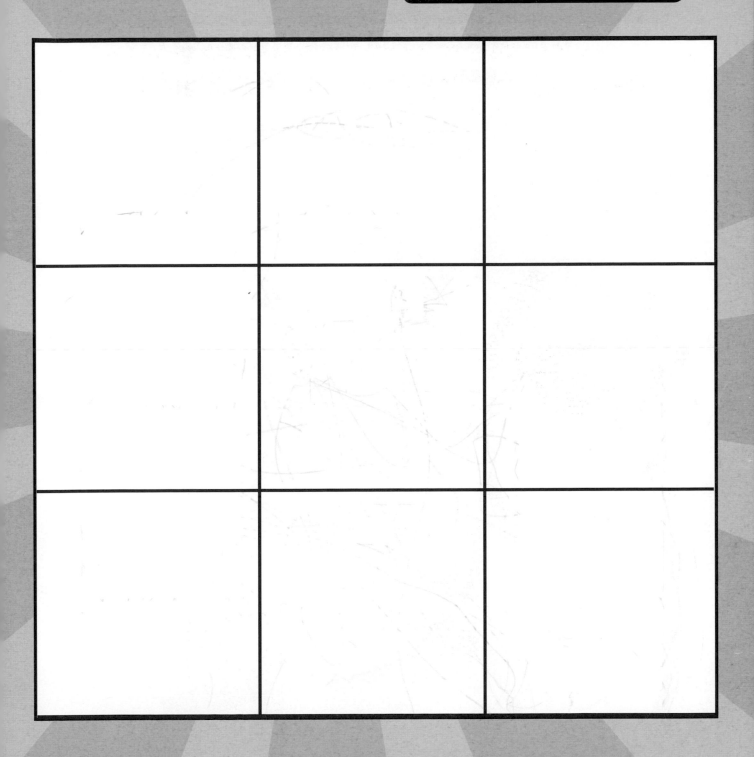

Recycling yard

Which track will take Wilson to the recycling yard to help Irving?

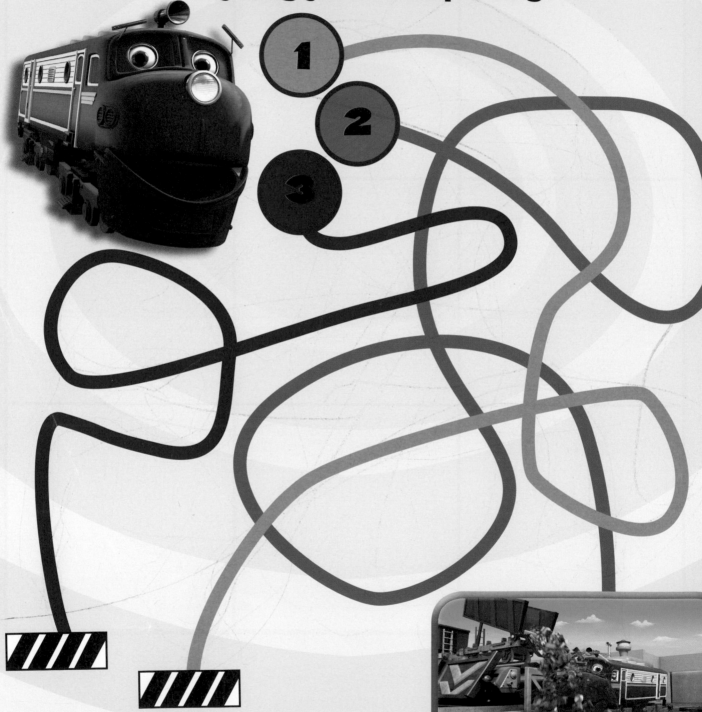

1

2

3

Can you connect the dots 1-10 to complete this picture of Action Chugger? Then colour him in!

Night run

Koko has broken down during a night run, and Brewster has to tow her! Follow Brewster through the maze to get Koko home.

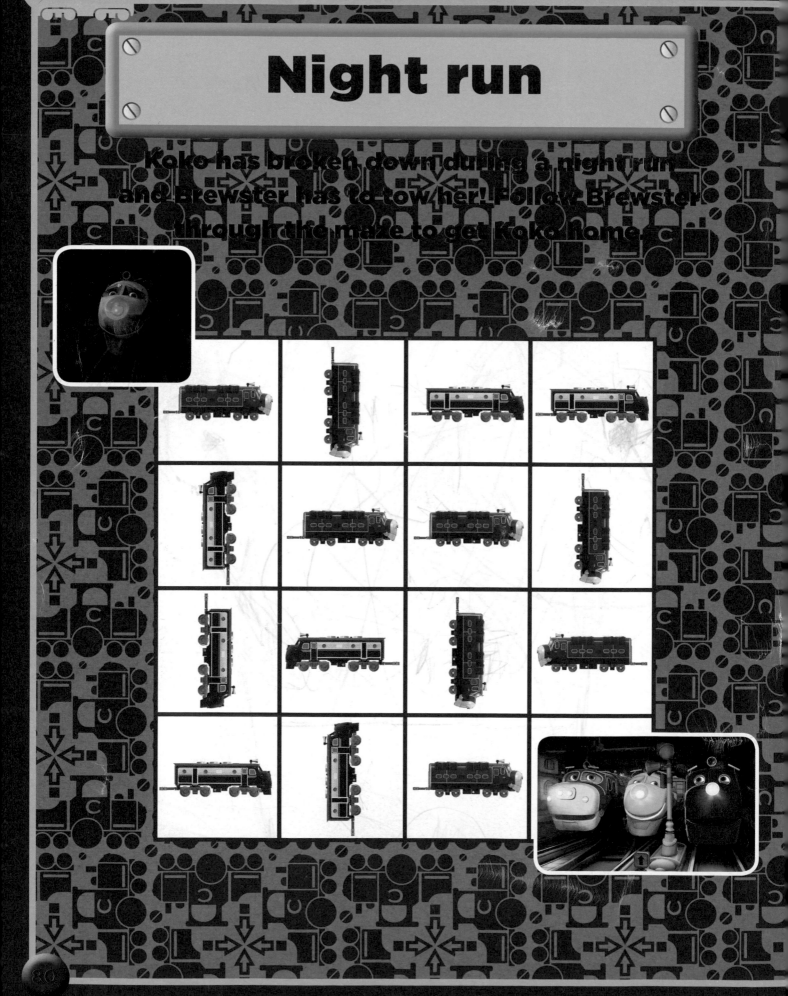

Missing pieces

Can you draw lines to connect the correct pieces to the big picture?

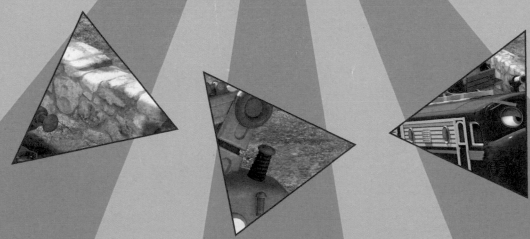

Ticket time

 1 What time is Dunbar going to the quarry?

_____ o'clock

 2 What time is Calley going to the safari park?

_____ o'clock

 3 What time is Harrison going to the chuggwash?

_____ o'clock

What time do the chuggers need to go to each location?

4 What time is Koko going to the docks?

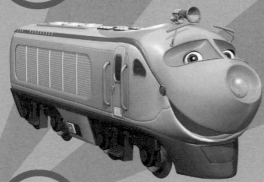  

_____ o'clock

5 What time is Brewster going to the farm?

_____ o'clock

6 What time is Wilson going to the repair shed?

_____ o'clock

ZEPHIE'S ZOOMAROUND

One morning, Brewster and Zephie were going to the farm. A new lamb needed some special feed.

After a while, Brewster started to get annoyed with Zephie, who was talking all the time.
"We're turning now," Brewster said, bored.
"I'm really good at turning!" Zephie said. But when she stopped spinning she found out she was alone!

Zephie didn't like being alone and started to get worried.
She rang her bell, but it was too quiet for anyone to hear.
Then Olwin chugged along the track.
"I was looking for the new lamb, but I got lost," Zephie told her,
feeling very sorry for herself.

Olwin took Zephie to the repair shed, where Morgan fixed her
with a siren. When she turned it on, it flashed and made a loud
noise. Morgan warned her that the siren was just for emergencies,
like if she got lost again.

Outside the repair shed, Zephie found it fun to keep trying out her siren.

"Make sure it's an emergency Zephie," Eddie laughed when he realised she was just playing.

Zephie zoomed around Chuggington, searching for an emergency.

At the recycling yard, Zephie thought she heard a growling noise. Then she saw some danger signs!

Scared that a lion had escaped from the safari park, she quickly set off her siren.

Dunbar sped into the recycling yard to see what the emergency was. Suddenly the growling noise stopped and Irving emerged from behind a wall. The noise had been Irving snoring!
"You mustn't let your imagination ride away with you," Dunbar said sternly.

Zephie carried on looking for an emergency so she could use her siren. At the park, she saw a squirrel in a tree. The squirrel wasn't moving! It must be stuck! "Help! Help!" she called, setting off the siren.

Eddie rushed over and told her that the squirrel lived in the tree. It wasn't stuck at all!

"I don't think you're quite ready for a siren yet Zephie," he said, taking it away.

Zephie felt very sad without her siren and was sorry she had set if off so much. She decided to go and meet the lamb. The lamb was very happy to see someone new and bleated hello.
"Hello! I mean...baaaaa..." Zephie replied happily.
"I can talk lamb!" she giggled.

Zephie was so excited about the lamb she jumped up and spun around. But then she fell over and couldn't get up! Zephie tried and tried, but she was stuck.
"If only I had my siren!" she yelped. Felix the farmer found Zephie and quickly telephoned for Calley to come and help.

Calley was able to get Zephie ready to ride the rails again, and brought the little chugger back to the repair shed. Morgan gave her siren back.
"I promise, I'll only use it for real emergencies from now on!" Zephie giggled.

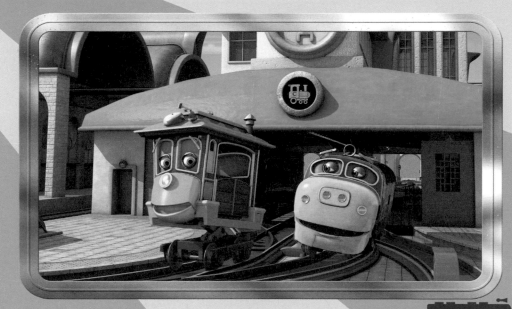

Chugger spotting

Can you spot the names in the grid below?
Looks forwards, back, up and down!

B	O	I	P	R	V	E
R	K	V	F	K	G	L
E	C	E	M	D	J	F
W	Z	E	O	A	B	T
S	H	H	A	O	R	D
T	B	J	Q	K	U	Y
E	E	W	H	X	O	Z
R	N	A	G	R	O	M

MORGAN

VEE

HODGE

BREWSTER

Answers

PAGE 8
The yellow tunnel

Page 9

PAGE 10
Brewster - 4
Koko - 4
Wilson - 4

PAGE 25
Koko - 3 sacks
Wilson - 4 sacks
Brewster - 5 sacks

PAGE 26
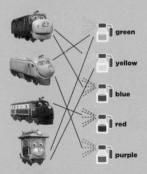

PAGE 27

PAGE 28-29
1 - red
2 - the safari park
3 - 3
4 - ice-cream
5 - Traintastic

PAGE 36

PAGE 41

PAGE 42

PAGE 45
Track 3

PAGE 46-47

PAGE 54
Hodge and Eddie 4

PAGE 58
1   2   3

PAGE 59

PAGE 60-61

The time is 9 o'clock

PAGE 62

DEWSTER

WILBER

COOKIE

PAGE 63

Zephie
Vee
Olwin
Harrison
Chatsworth
Emery

PAGE 64

Page 65

Page 72
The blue tunnel

Page 73

Page 78
Track 2

Page 80

Page 81

Page 82
1 - 10 o'clock
2 - 3 o'clock
3 - 9 o'clock
4 - 2 o'clock
5 - 1 o'clock
6 - 6 o'clock

PAGE 90

B	O	I	P	R	V	E
R	K	V	F	K	G	L
E	C	E	M	D	J	F
W	Z	E	O	A	B	T
S	H	H	A	O	R	D
T	B	J	Q	K	U	Y
E	E	W	H	X	O	Z
R	N	A	G	R	O	M

CHUGGINGTON™

Complete your Chuggington collection.
Tick them off as you collect!

More chuggtastic books to collect!

CLUNKY WILSON
ISBN 978-1-4075-6041-0

CAN'T CATCH KOKO
ISBN 978-1-4075-6042-7

BRAKING BREWSTER
ISBN 978-1-4075-8009-8

WAKE UP WILSON!
ISBN 978-1-4075-8010-4

KOKO AND THE TUNNEL
ISBN 978-1-4075-9530-6

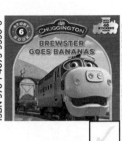
BREWSTER GOES BANANAS
ISBN 978-1-4075-9531-3

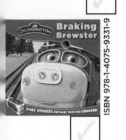
Braking Brewster
ISBN 978-1-4075-9331-9

Clunky Wilson
ISBN 978-1-4075-9332-6

Hodge and the Magnet
ISBN 978-1-4075-9333-3

Koko and the Squirrels
ISBN 978-1-4075-9334-0

Wilson Gets a Wash
ISBN 978-1-4075-9335-7

Zephie's Zoomaround
ISBN 978-1-4075-9336-4

COPY COLOUR POSTER BOOK
ISBN 978-1-4075-6126-4

STICKER SCENE STORY
ISBN 978-1-4075-6044-1

Bumper Sticker Book
ISBN 978-1-4075-8141-5

POSTER BOOK
GIANT PULL-OUT POSTER
ISBN 978-1-4075-9529-0

ACTIVITY BOOK
WITH 6 CHUGGER PUZZLES
ISBN 978-1-4075-9422-4
Little library

MY FIRST LITTLE LIBRARY
ISBN 978-1-4075-6043-4

Construct and Play!
ISBN 978-1-4075-9882-6

MEET THE CHUGGERS
ISBN 978-1-4075-9884-0
Annual

ANNUAL 2011
LET'S RIDE THE RAILS!
ISBN 978-1-84535-437-4
Activity pack

CHUGGER TRAVEL PACK
ISBN 978-1-4075-9885-7
3D books

3D
ISBN 978-1-4075-8349-5

ISBN 978-1-4075-9780-5
Chugger Sticker Colouring Pad

SING AND LEARN
ISBN 978-1-4075-6127-1

KOKO ON CALL
ISBN 978-1-4075-8142-2
Story collection

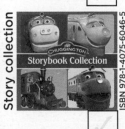
Storybook Collection
ISBN 978-1-4075-6046-5
Train books

WILSON
LET'S RIDE THE RAILS!
ISBN 978-1-4075-8138-5

KOKO
CHUGGA CHUGGA CHOO CHOO!
ISBN 978-1-4075-8139-2

BREWSTER
HONKING HORNS!
ISBN 978-1-4075-8140-8